Radio Sphere
Devin terSteeg

Dedication

Just as from Niflheim there arose a
coldness and all things grim, so what
was facing close to Muspell was hot and
bright, but Ginnungagap was as mild as a
windless sky. And when rime and the blowing
warmth met so that it thawed and dripped,
there was a quickening from these
flowing drops due to the power
source of heat, and it became
the form of a man, and he was
given the name
Xmir.

.

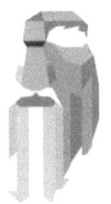

Radio Sphere

Devin ter Steeg

Rime Giant

www.RimeGiant.com

First published by Rime Giant.
First printing, May 2015

ISBN: 0692489444
ISBN-13: 978-0692489444

This book, honestly, is for me.
Thank you for reading.

.

Contents

Zero   1

49.5 Part 1   3

Zero   26

Saraswati   29

Zero   37

Elizabeth's Westward Journey   39

Zero   53

George's Transient Downturn   55

Zero   78

49.5 Part 2 – Elizabeth   80

The Last Balloon   110

Zero Again   123

Zero[1]

Forbearer-

I am unsure how well received this letter will be. I understand that emotions- outright outrage and terrible frustrations- are all we parted with. I hope time has devoured our sins.

It was difficult for me to say goodbye to our planet's timber skies, truth be told, despite what false front I'd managed at the

---

1. "Not many years back we learned the news that the Lebagir are not alone," he paused. "We all gathered together, huddled with our friends and family, to hear the sounds broadcast through the stars that found their way to our Timber planets. That is somehow old news now, as the first images from the alien world have been processed by the ᴣᴸᴎ¥ᴊℵ telecomputer. A resplendent world like none we've seen, sitting all alone, blue like a polished stone." The newscaster won an award for his historic commentary. He went on to discuss the implications there would be on our society, namely in terms of religion and science, since for many the proof of another species provided the last evidence their dogma was correct. The eruption of chaos combined with cold rationale of the movement's leaders forced action from every group with an opinion and will to act. Nobody wanted any particular result except to be accepted as in the right. It made little sense, those days, so many of the scientists and engineers behind the initial discoveries grouped and lost in exile to construct our passage.

time. The inescapable, constant hum of
machines and solid black out the windows
once frightened me greatly. Our destination
is the effulgent blue pearl; their solar
system is not much different from others
we've observed. Now I'm actually happy to be
out here, our people were never much for
exploration and now I can see why; the
depths of space are severely lonely. I keep
remembering why we left and I am sorry it
pushed us apart.

Great hope and wonder now fills me.

These Refulgent Creatures hold many
mysteries. I'm excited to meet them! Each
day I try to imagine a little about how they
think, what they value, what they enjoy. How
far have they come since the transmissions
we've seen? How fictional are the scenes
they play out? While traveling at such great
speeds we are unable to certify any
transmissions since we left.

How bottomless *is* the chasm of
perspective we can learn from them, and the
other way around?

— With love,
ÀꝪꝊꝆꝊꝅ

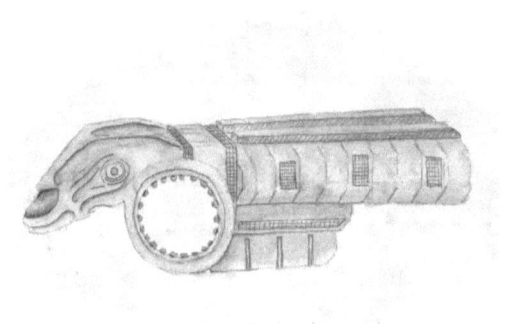

49.5 Part 1 [2]

I had a dream that I was making love to a woman in the bath tub. Her face was familiar, somehow, but I could not place it. The water was warm, right out of the tap. It wasn't candle but electric light illuminating the room. She started apologizing because, she said, only now did she start to find me attractive and I ignored her because I was busy. Thrusting

---

2. I had thought about "Ginger Jar in Fiction" but that felt pretentious, a weary vestige of my old 'self' as it might be called, to be conscious of something in a negative way. Then I'd have to go on about what ginger is, but I'm sure you've seen Gilligan's Island by now and that's good enough. Could have gone with "A wind beaten tree" but, these things... Fiction, though, has different uses for them. Humans escape in it, but use the escape to reaffirm prioritized traits and feelings. It makes sense to me actually.

and grunting, but that was automatic, I was busy reflecting on the history of this room. It was my bathroom and at the same time not. Colorful blue and orange sunset wallpaper covered everything and the tub still stood on its feet. She got offended, but what could I do? There was no blood to lubricate my dream-thoughts, there was only an instinctual command line that resonated through me that demanded a child come from this union. Instinctual, but yet I wondered how the walls looked so clean and bright unlike anything I'd ever seen before. She got out of the tub.

"Just because we can fit together," she said as the water and soap bubbles cascaded down from her lopsided breasts, "doesn't mean we are a team to fight injustice or both wear skirts."

Now I recognized her, Samantha from work and she was beautiful down to the scar that tore through her left thigh and curved to the top of the butt cheek on the same side stopping short of her spine.

We hadn't finished, and my brain

4

demanded at least some of the blood back to figure out why. Samantha walked into the hallway, into the bedroom, then locked herself in the closet to cry, which was ironic to me because she had wanted a doorless walk-in style closet but that might have been a different dream. As she walked across the carpet, all I could think of was those droplets of water still falling from her curves would find their way down into the long fibers to discover ancient dust and commingle into mud.

I awoke in my ecru colored world with its painted blood-brown walls and I felt like a *woman on her deathbed*, and I was Elizabeth again. I didn't choose the decor. Out my window, the Boston sky was the color of raw cinnamon, as it always was. It was a million degrees because I rented this old couple's attic, and through the center of the room scorched a chimney that mathematically meant I never got cold up there. They always kept a fire going, my rented old people, who owned and operated a museum in their retirement out of the old

Faneuil Hall, in nearly everything else they were sparse.

It was delightful to be in my own skin again, even if it was barely sub-volcanic, because I had grand plans that I needed to get to if I was going to make it to mom and dad's before curfew.[3]

I started the day by retracing the path my dream woman- I meant the woman from my dream, not the woman *of* my dreams- Samantha, took from the tan tiled bathroom with painted, not wallpapered, walls decorated by my old people with Jesus[4] sayings and cleaned at least seven times weekly by me. I got really excited because a few months after moving in I started working on a disinfectant to purify my home, and it was nearing perfection. I think I was weirded out; it was strange because I was a man in my dream... but stranger? She called me Sarah which isn't even my name.

---

3. Imposed house confinement during the times the star is down, which is rather vague, reminds me of home a bit at the end. We'd caused an uproar, a d20 of rebellion or revolution- mostly some loud groups making the lives stuck between them miserable. We thought ourselves noble.
4. A central character in a Refulgent belief structure known for his skill in painting eggs.

I was given a record player seven months ago for my nineteenth birthday and moving out present from Chad with a few 45s,[5] so I took the Bowie Earthling album I'd been listening to a lot over the last week off and put on Nena's 99 Luftballons, whoever had it before had been a fan of German[6] stuff, other albums included In Trance by Scorpions and Somewhere Far Beyond by Blind Guardian. If I were a boy I'd want to be called Anslem or Marcel or Tholand because those names sound strong.

The carpet could not have been defiled by a dream, but I scrubbed it with diluted hot vinegar mixed with nahcolite and ethanol for twenty-five minutes anyway. It's not like I could just get a new carpet.

Ever since the simultaneous nuclear

---

5. An ancient type of data- in this case musical- storage that self-destructs into a ball of fire after forty-five uses for the purpose of fire starting. Old timey Refulgents were inventive, for primitives.
6. In the before times, antediluvian humans developed along different ethnic paths with national segregations. One of these was called German, a pride known for its blond hair and advanced chocolate engineering.

detonations above the clouds[7] people have been strange, Grandpa says, like never before. The result of the explosions in the upper atmosphere knocked out most of the electronics as far as Monsantonia,[8] Grandpa knew all about it and most of what devices survived seemed random to me. I didn't use a lot of electricity, so I never had to worry about using up my power rations, plus I had the hand crank.

I spent five hours at The Laundromat playing DS,[9] I mean washing clothes, but I finished a ton of Yoshi's Island[10] and just felt awful accomplished. The only remaining

---

7. Located somewhat central, east coast, and western North America respectively; the former catacombs of human civilization called Chicago, Virginia Beach, and Reno were once populated, livable, and not completely terrifying. The radiation has died down, but the fallout and fear keeps most life away.
8. Includes what was once called Alaska, the Yukon province, and parts of the Northwest Territories.
9. A hand-held, portable game device created by the Responsibility Heaven Corporation (RHC)- which is exactly what it sounds like, a powerful technology conglomerate and plush toy manufacturer- primarily in use by under-parented children and lonely adults. The device underwent many variations until in 20XX a pill, once swallowed, enabled the brain to act as screen and controller as directed by the user's thoughts. It came out the day before we came and sold over 200 million units.
10. Dinosaur, the name Refulgents gave to their once living giant lizard overlords, long extinct before we got here, saves world with baby on board.

washateria in Boston looked like an old
homeless city, an outdoor sprawl of rusted
machines lit by torches[11] and covered by
whatever tarps they could find. The oxidized
washers filled the Common[12] in jagged clumps
that ran off generators brought in by Logan
at the end of each month. A large sign
posted exchange prices for goods- ethanol,
water at various qualities, grain, fuel and
workers. It was difficult to focus on the
game at times because this clunker of a
dryer sounded like it was popping giant
kernels of popcorn. I had to keep getting up
to switch loads and fold because I hadn't
washed clothes in three months, kept
noticing this guy with sunken eyes in a
gaunt face watching me fold as if I were
teaching him how; he thought I didn't notice
him studying me until I mistakenly looked up
and caught his eye.

"I'm leaving at three to go pick

---

11. Before the commercialization of incendiary weapons, a
class of which is called the Torch, any flammable material
such as a rag wrapped around a stick could have been called a
torch.
12. A central Boston nature-park built before flora became
obsolete to the humans.

apples,"[13] he said.

I returned a self-comforting smile.

The place alone gave me goosebumps, it had a disquiet that was easy to mistakenly overlook- hundreds of people all around yet alone, so I was glad to have some clean clothes and could leave. That creeper was easy enough to ignore the rest of the time even though I knew he kept staring at me.

Mom and dad had me over for dinner, I hadn't seen them in seven months, since moving out, but most importantly Chad would be there. Chad had these pectoral muscles that must have been so comfortable to lean into, to fall asleep on, that he could use to protect me. His hair had this one brawny

---

13. Prior to the Great-paste Nutra-meal suppositories most enjoyed today, the Earth's past had a large variety of food that provided inadequate nourishment unless combined with many other variants. Most likely the "apple" was a food of vibrant color, possibly yellow, and was known to cause prolonged sleep which was the Refulgent's ancestors only method of keeping illness at bay. Yes, all the movies that showed the fruit had been, coincidentally, destroyed, thus relegating the "apple" as nothing more than a myth.

Superman[14] curl that danced around his forehead as he moved and he had that faux-mountainous[15] smell of a clean man. My own One from City of Lost Children.[16]

Chad got along well with my dad ever since his own father passed- which meant he started going over to our house. I could see in dad's eyes a calm he never had years ago whenever he and Chad had their long mentorus talks in the study. Chad was only four years older than me. Mom, who was pushing 232 years old, and birthed me at 213, grew up with Chad's dad back before the world changed from blue to brown. We figured mom was among the last still alive- from before the bombs went off- in Boston at least.

I completed more of Yoshi's Island, sitting on the duffel of clean clothes,

---

14. Character from one of the types of books people have the patience to read, due to its colorful illustrations and breezy readability. It is also from one of the first quality transmissions we encountered; my name is taken from the hero's intelligent and beautiful human friend. Although we look dissimilar to humans, unlike the Superman himself, we had hoped for a similar friendship and mutual cooperation.
15. Old Spice, it's from a different planet. Loeshiob, I think.
16. That was Ron Pearlman according to the last great repository of human knowledge called IMDb.

while I waited for the T[17] which came late
because it had been stalled by another
jumper-[18] people having trouble coping with
one thing or another. The trains only ran
for three hours in the morning and again for
three hours in the evening, so jumpers
completely messed up the schedule.

Mom once told me that people looted
until they realized the TVs they'd stolen
wouldn't work, after that there wasn't a lot
of crime. Mom had said it was better now,
that I could live happily, but I could tell
she always missed something from before. She
almost never spoke about what it was like in
her youth.

Logan had men there, lifting, moving,
hammering; they all wore jumpsuits of
mismatched colors- green, orange, blue- and
operated in ordered groups of four or five.
The colors didn't seem to correspond to
anything at all. Nobody spoke to them and
they spoke to nobody, the men with guns

17. Local terminological word usage for the metro subway that
runs through Boston, derived from the word "trap" because
many of the seedy elements of the Refulgent's society
utilized it for their benefit over law abiding folk.
18. Someone jumped. The train stopped. You get the idea.

watched from all corners. The men with guns usually patrolled on foot between, and at, the train stations.

From the John courthouse, Boylston, Dartmouth, and down to Union Park the soldiers made triangular patrol routes. You could see them clearly from high enough- when reading The Giver on the topmost accessible floor of the remains of John Hancock Tower- I could watch the clusters of dots blithely roam.

Some jumpsuit men came from down track with plastic gloves and containers covered with tarps or canvas or something.

Even after the Callahan tunnel collapsed Logan kept regular patrols and the general appearance of order. Grandpa and dad worked very hard to hold the city together; each held high positions at one time. They kept the city from ruin.

Greater Boston became a figurative island, surrounded by a sea of chaos and ignorance, except the occasional caravans that came in through Mass Pike from nowhere towns not on the old maps.

The trucks were like clothing; scraps
stitched together and lumbering around like
Frankenstein's monster- things that didn't
seem to fit in the world.

The trucks were cobbled together from
Logan's hoarded tires; most had a bed built
from a picnic table and children's park
equipment since all they needed to do was
haul Great-paste from where ever they were
grown.

I watched the trucks because they
rumbled and made no sense. How can piles of
debris be energized to life- they were more
than the sum of their parts and had a great
usefulness- but were nothing like Wenji and
her family. Of the eight trucks- Kitahn,
Copley, Perry, Shaw, Lowry, Nena, Hepburn,
and Dean- that motored about the city from
time to time, Nena was my favorite. She had
two silver slides on her side to wall the
back of the truck and monkey bars that
soldiers would dangle their legs through to
gate the hatch. Nena limped the most and,
when the soldier's would remove the plastic
green turtle shell of a hood to see and fix

14

what may have gone wrong, she was loved the most by her companions.

The soldiers who drive the trucks brought news bulletins and announcements from Logan, posted in public areas. The thin paper sheets and paint-like ink rendered the missives lives short, so most communities had a reader or two to relay the news.

I kept records at the water dispensary, they'd set us up in Old South Church, which wasn't too far a walk from my apartment. Many of the old churches were converted into water dispensaries since running water had been cut off to the city two centuries ago due to contamination, radiation. It was supposed to be clean water. The serosity was impure. I'd often watch the particles float in the water and dance across sunlight and wonder what they were. It had to be something gross; from a dead fish, frog poop, mud, or human bits.

We kept handwritten records on paper, so we had a sizable staff to keep everything organized and accounted for. The city had re-purposed a lot of space around the financial district for workers to make paper, ink, and other necessities. Grandpa taught me cursive, but those weren't allowed at work because nobody could read them. Handwriting died out at least two generations ago- we revived it; we were chosen because our hand-eye coordination allowed for the most legible writing in Boston. I got fed for working; it beat some of the other jobs people needed doing. Grandpa taught me most of my lessons growing up since he was already retired and lived with us, he was one of the few to have lived for over 300[19] years. He was a leader at Logan, an archivist, a strategist, the last of a certain type of educated man, a teacher. Dad told me there used to be a time, long ago, when people craved the knowledge to read and write, but that even

---

19. As the elderly quickly lost cognitive functionality old world knowledge was lost. I have learned that the 20 billion world population, with lifespans averaging 350 years, drastically dropped. In the 200 years since our unpleasant arrival, Greater Boston is now home to just under a quarter million raggedy souls, with average lifespans under 70 years. Like children climbing a tower higher and higher into the sky, not knowing it was luck alone holding them to the tower-side, the Refulgents grew in confidence, like a seemingly solitary act, they believed it was nothing but their right to climb higher still. They weren't wrong.

Grandpa wasn't old enough to have seen it. The whole city was saddened by Grandpa's decline, how the radiation affected his memory, and the medicine that allowed for his extended life began to run out causing rapid decay and irreparable aging. The same happened to mom, the supplies at Mass General[20] waned, the last reserved for those already on the treatment. They won't get enough- no more was going to come- causing synaptic function to decrease more than anything physical, the older you were the harsher the decline. The elders became husks, first like children, then like barely living mannequins until they finally died.

When the T came I put away my DS and entered the screeching car. They're kind of amazing. The whole subway smelled of the old world; sun and rust and rain; the green and gray cars looks like they've traveled it whole.

I lugged the duffel into the center of

---

20. Massachusetts General Hospital lasted about a hundred and eighty years until it, as the elderly Refulgents themselves had, became foul- still water and mold; a reek like cold vomit- as it would slowly die and be forgotten.

the train car. The creeper from the laundromat had followed me. They say the sudden emptiness of the world had affected people's brains, Grandpa called them beat-brains; most of the people who were badly affected had already died off, but some still lived and their brains flow like an icebound river. They can't even figure out basic Van Hiele,[21] then suddenly they can see things we can't, insights and the like, as if their brains were reconstructed in a different way- a broken yet beautiful calamity. Grandpa came across many in his time working at Logan and he was one, in a way, as he died. They all were, the aged ones, as they no longer got the medicines that kept them.

He coughed like he wanted to keep even the air out, but gave up for a while because his body made him; try, try again.

"Don't you what I know regret toast?"

---

21. "The student learns by rote to operate with mathematical relations that he does not understand, and of which he has not seen the origin"... and all that. These creatures tend to name things after the person who brought a concept to popular attention. You could make a very complicated series of Eulerian circles to depict this.

Grandpa muttered to his own photograph from ninety years before. He giggled to himself, took a sip of water that dribbled down his shirt, and flicked the photo across the room with a tear in his eye.

In his younger elderly years, he was often harsh and cold because he wanted more from people and they rarely lived up to his expectations. He didn't care about how you did something but, rather why you did it- if you messed up constantly for the right reasons he came close to giving you a pass.

"I do like toast, don't you miss it Lizzie?" I wasn't sure what toast was I just placated him and he rocked back and forth with a grin. I picked up his photograph and he asked me what I had in my hand.

"It's a kind of bird, Grandpa, have you've seen these kind before?"

"Oh yes, long ago we had a bird bath in our yard and those and all kinds of birds hopped on all fours... they bathed and dad shot them with pellets. I thought them all extinct, didn't you Iola?"

We were alone so I knew he forgot I

wasn't my mother, but it wasn't the first time so I knew not to fight back. Things got bad when I didn't play along.

"Well Grandpa, if these birds are so rare maybe we can follow them home- maybe there are more there and we can go on an adventure."

"I'm too old for adventure."

"One last adventure!"

"You're too young to leave the house."

"That's the thing you remember?"

"Where is your mother? Sarah? Sarah?!"

"Sarah's not my mom. Who is Sarah?"

"Sarah?!"

The spittle flew from his mouth because he knew Sarah was dead, but he also thought she was in the next room. My mother heard his shouts and joined us.

"Papa, it's me- Iola."

"I know that. You're right over there," he pointed at me.

"That's Liz, your granddaughter, Papa,"

"Yes, little Lizzie. That's right." He leaned in and whispered "Lizzie and I are going on an adventure. She thinks the photo is a bird."

The boy from the laundromat kept staring at me, and soon I could smell the mix of fecal and mint odors he carried with him.

"They're not green, your sister saw the sky that isn't hers- threw a seahorse at them all!"

I mistakenly giggled.

"Hush! The plum poppies don't know *anything* yet."

He descended upon me with his aggression palpable, almost condensing on the windows. The enclosed train car left me with no place to escape to. He held a red, uneaten apple[22] in one hand hanging off a limp arm as he raised the other hand above his head. The train cart rocked gently as it rolled down the track and I ran to the door. I got as far away from him as I could, my

---

22. The apple is no longer a myth. I think. Or do I mean illusion. Which is important and which gives importance. It's definitely not an allegory. Fruit can often be thought of as juice, or flesh, but the best is when it comes in those little gummy candies. Wait, you don't know about those? Don't lose track, not now. Apples are grown from seeds, like people, but unlike people they grow in trees. People climb trees. Trees are smarter.

back to the wall, he still stood on the other side of the car looking at me with a gloss over his eyes that I'd seen in Grandpa's eyes that meant nobody was home. The door was locked. There were no other people on the Earth, for a single moment; I was alone with erratic behavior personified.

"I didn't mean anything by it," I pleaded.

"Find your way."

I wanted to escape, to find someone who could help, to float away into the sky on a cloud. I had to stall until the next station, to keep myself present at this of all moments. I couldn't remember how far it was; panic infiltrated my perception like black-water drops running down a window with cascading intensity blurring my vision. The train car got smaller as the man got closer. I wondered how much was my fault.

I shouldn't have looked at him at the laundromat.

I shouldn't have giggled.

I shouldn't have gotten out of bed today.

I pretended like I was in control by hiding secret power in my soul, waiting, waiting, waiting for Chad to notice me and see that every day- most days for no reason at all- I live, and it is due only to my secret difference from everyone else, this uniqueness in my soul. That I could, at any moment of my choosing, release my power. I looked the creeper in the eyes, the eyes reminded me I had no power but more of a hope that, because I'm alone, I struggle to hold on to.

He stopped his advance and struggled to express: "...because it's donut day,"

"I forgive you," for being a beat-brain. It wasn't his fault for being that way; broken and lost in his own mind. I was almost happy to be there beside him, but that's only because I realized how much alike he was to anyone else, really, lost in the weird world of mental states covered in dirt and grime with no clean perch to rest on. "...so please don't hurt me."

He lunged at me. In an awkward arc, he fell forward as if he were defying gravity and stayed there impossibly for several moments. The train was slowing. It allowed him to hold an absurd stance before tripping over my duffel and falling on his back. His long messy hair covering his sunken eyes, he cried. I left the train. Left my DS on the seat. I'd got off several stops too early. Some stranger would find out that Yoshi's Island was my escape, and they'll steal it for themselves: that wonderful island, shiny and clean, where I actually had my hidden power. I ran away from the station. My mind was blank. I didn't realize I was running until a raw taste filled my mouth then faded away. I shook in that inside part of me that knows reality and keeps me there even when I most want to go crazy. I try to escape and live in a butterfly world with old world foods because this is a place where nobody cares and we all grow fat and live happily. It could be a place where nothing decayed and all day and night was sunny.

The wind blew flecks of rust, as it often had, that danced like I'd imagined ballerinas did. I ducked into the museum to wait out the storm. Faneuil Hall was all but abandoned, two elderly creatures prowled the building to dust off the artifacts they'd collected there. Most of it was tech that no longer functioned, but stacked in piles that looked artistic. A pile of television guts here, the screens over there, black and gray cases and whatnots on whatnots. Rome, I've seen in pictures, had marble statues and we have these.

I went back to the crowded station an hour later to catch the 6pm train the rest of the way to my parent's neighborhood. A malodorous emanation lingered in the train that may or may not have been real.

ℨero

62/4-9;

Three of the senior staff woke up from stasis today. Three! The system has been and continues to experience errors- only 5 Ly from port- faster than I can get ahead of them. This technology was highly experimental to begin with, we have no idea the long term consequences these errors will have on the bodies that are continually forced back and forth. These issues should have all been worked on more before we left. There is not much point if we arrive with a ship full of corpses. We do not have half enough supplies to ride out of stasis for the remaining journey.

Our ship, The Great Reeves leaves much to be desired as we watch our home-star shrink behind us, luckily for me and everyone aboard this ship ⟨⟩⟨⟩⟨⟩⟨⟩ has endless enthusiasm for her job and never seems to sleep. Picking her for my second-in-command has been most beneficial.

— ⟨⟩⟨⟩⟨⟩⟨⟩K

Announcements:

It has come to my attention that several system errors have occurred in the past few cycles. Even my own stasis has malfunctioned several times. Things are under control now thanks to the hard work of ЧЧÐŒ¥ and his team. Things are bound to go wrong from time to time considering the size of the flotilla and the population in stasis, operations are essentially nominal.

Have you been wondering how things are back home? Lately, I've been experiencing headaches and miss the tea made by my grandmother that always quelled the pain.

Have they completely adjusted to our departure? I hope that everything is settled back home, that passions have died down and that peace exists again. Many of our crew have messages to send to their families back home and we can only hope they will accept them. Please contact ȦҮÐⱮO℔ if you have a message to add to the stream.

We've managed to maintain a steady velocity at roughly 1/4c for several... for 20 years now. The 232-year trip, we still believe it to be worth it. The lings of Earth do not pose any threat to our species, our religion, or our culture. Our two species are not mutually exclusive of each other, as some believe. They may have their own ideas, but together we can forge a stronger future. I hope we all see that. I want something like that written for my epitaph.

I hope my daughter, ЧЧÐŒ¥, is doing well with her mother and uncles- that all those we love and left behind experienced no

undue hardship because of us. Ok, let's end
the message there. Thank you, back to work
everyone.

—   Zeal Prime

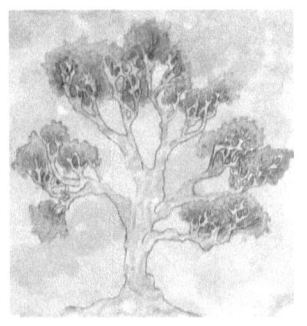

Saraswati

"George,[23] wake up," the nature all around me seemed to say, but waking up is merely a process by which ones' consciousness resumes; lightening to scare the gerbils back to work. The world cannot speak. Blinking, my eyes had to readjust to solar illumination. Spending several hours in a tenebrific imagination and subconscious

---

23. The second specimen, George, had a stranger set of experiences many of which his brain believes are perfectly real, but even I have a hard time taking them at face value. Then again, Refulgents have silly ways this alien planet is downright fascinating. For instance, their science has a sect called psychiatry. They try to, and often with success, analyses and understand each others emotions and dreams, their species is subject to a great and fascinating number of mental illnesses. They seem not to be able to understand a vast deal of their own mental chemistries, yet can manage to observe cause and effect to the acute degree of accurate remedy. Detrimentally, they fail to apply such reasoning to other aspects of their societies.

world eaten up by nothing is nice, stuck with a billion beveled thoughts, but knowing that here I'm supposed to be alone is how I keep moving. It is more difficult to be alone when I'm awake, where I'm just George and am always stuck *here*. I enjoy dreams, even if they are scary because they take me to other places and I can meet all kinds of people.

So I rolled over and back to reverie for a few months.

I woke up to a gradient brown welkin as the sun rose amongst low hanging billowing shapes that looked like cooking pans and cats, for a while, then the wind started, and all the white was streaked across the browns-on-brown sky leaving me cloudless on my journey. "George," pa'd said, "the whole world is change." I instantly knew he meant it, but didn't know how so until years later.

The rhythmic repeats of the world became plain to us after so much walking- cold then warm happens during a day but over a course of days as well- then alone I

returned to the city where I was born
feeling like I could die at any moment. I
met mom and pa here for the first time. My
baggage was so heavy I was forced to gently
place it on the ground and rest at least a
week before picking it back up. There is a
tree, I remember it from child times, behind
the gray, tall walls that pa spent all that
time patching. When I found it that morning,
I knew. I was home.

The tree had grown, as I had, and now
is several devrons tall and sprawling like a
Hindu goddess with her arms stretching in
all directions. The beauty of the tree I had
long missed was a deep, almost emerald,
green abundant with the reddest pomaceous
fruit. I couldn't be sure if it had all been
just a dream until then. It was the only
thing left in all the yard. The house became
like bones in a pile picked of all their
meat. While devouring countless apples, I
had a discussion with Vishnu.

"Haven't you missed me?"

"I... recognize you."

"Yes, absolutely. You'll talk!"

"It has been a long time, boy, since anybody has come around here, hugging a commode and coughing up blood, and seeing the blood spurt everywhere was a fly gasping out of fear while perched within my branches."

I ate, and as I did I became a man. A human one. Something I had been struggling to remember how to be.

"You will mend some with time, but never gone, nor should you desire such, will the past be."

"I didn't meet many of your kind while I've been gone... none were quite like you."

"Staying alone without the woods, with the whispers of the trees as your only company, the lonesome nights come end to end, the shallow moon as your only light to find your way out of the dark. Look for the now. As your self is your friend. Your lostness will soon come to an end."

The Essence and I had found a sort of companionship over so long a time that my hair stopped growing. Through long lectures she sagaciously taught me about biology, astronomy, philosophy, along with reason and logic. She taught me how unwise I was and continued to be, and gave me the perspective to understand, to know the correct direction to pursue. She reminded me of many memories-through discussion, meditation, and the eating of apples.

Long ago during the time I was small, when mom and pa were still around, I had a vastly different life. We lived in a pleasant home, in Jamaica Plain with bay windows built above its garage into a small hill, all painted white. The front yard was filled with brick and cement sidewalk and stairway to the house. Mom would be inside cooking while overlooking me from the window while I played in the backyard within the tree's grasp. I had no friends as no others lived in the neighborhood. Pa scavenged what we needed. It always scared me when he'd come back with his rifle, smelling of the world the way I do now. My entire world was that walled in yard. Mom almost never left the house.

When I was seven, others came while pa

was away. I had climbed the highest I could get in the tree, my record height, before I knew her name: Saraswati; nearly two devrons up. I tried to see as far as I could but long ago someone built the wall to keep them safe, it hadn't, and I was too frightened to climb any higher and never could see over the top. I didn't know anything was wrong until the scream. Three men had broken through the front door, lured by the smell of something she had cooked, stabbed her, took the food. Pa came home late, after the setting sun, and I had stayed in the tree too scared to move, after too long unable to move, unwilling. He found me and we left.

We walked forever. We never found the men, if that's even what we were trying to do. We walked all over the brown, devoid coast, pa and I, always looking for something we could never find. That's what I thought at least, since he never said anything, probably there never was a search.

"Sometimes we just lose our anchor and drift," mom once told me, but pa would just tell her that the ships are all gone.

Pa never spoke about mom, about where we'd go, about anything at all for a long time. When he did start talking again, it was not at all like before. He was crooked, he told me that mom was pregnant when she was killed and that was only after we found a cache of something called Loch Lamond. I made a face each sip causing him to call me "Anacoluthon." He never took the time to heal, he was brokenhearted. I was 27 when I stopped wandering and finally found this home, and Saraswati, again.

I can't remember mom's name. Her face.

"At least for a time we had each other. The years pulled us onward and eventually pulled pa down to his last breath. I wasn't certain, but I figured pa was glad he could finally stop walking. He could go into the ground like mom. He told me I had to cover him with ground. He didn't spend those last years being my father, but he did teach me how to do what he did, how to clean the rifle that's now long broken, how to kill and clean an animal, how to cook it, how to make water drinkable. He taught me our family's name and how to write it. After a time, I tried to re-trace our wanderous path back. My only semblance of a goal, the only image in my mind, was you. When pa died I carried him back and put him into the hole like he wanted, next to mom's, then I was truly alone and didn't know what to do. It took me three months to travel from the hole in the front-yard to you in the back-yard."

It was just empty buildings. Everywhere I went. No people, few trees. I saw a few birds fly through the void we call the sky. Essentially alone, all the world pretended it was more than a faded ghost.

"You are not alone. We look at the same sky each night George, together or not, and we feel the warmth of the same sun."

I wanted to find another person. A companion or a friend. A sister or brother.

"The city hasn't changed much since you left, yet it has changed a lot."

"As long as there are people."

Zero

Forbearer-

　　During my downtime I've been watching a cataloged Refulgent program about an alien that has been orphaned on their planet. They have wonderful imaginations. Their image and exploration of alien life forms is intriguing if somewhat self-centered and flawed. We don't look exactly alike, nor did we assume we would, yet this interpretation they've devised has introduced me to a new concept. It seems that the alien is imbued with traits the Earthlings value most. Strength, resolute conviction, notions of upholding justice, protection of the weak. Mostly ideas we have parallels with, but curiously this Steel Man is willing to allow his own destruction and endure enormous pain to do what he believes is Right and to save people with no known value. For people he doesn't even know.

　　Refulgents certainly have much to teach us, to open us to, and I hope we can do the same for them. I fear we have no culture of significant value to them, but perhaps that is merely my own bias.

I've taken to a character from the show called Lois Lane. The superman is not very much like us, but I feel that this Lois embodies a curiosity much like we started this mission with. We don't operate through strength and power, but explore with truth trying to discover the new and interesting. When we finally meet the Refulgents I will use the name to help facilitate our friendship; Lois Lane.

—   ÀꝪÐꝥOꝘ

Elizabeth's
Westward Journey

People always asked me: "Liz, where do you sit?" but I kept my options open.

I hate couches. When sitting on a couch I feel like it sucks me in, like into the crease in the back. If I sit on one for too long it feels like I'm folding in on myself and eventually I'll fold down to nothing, or something near to that. It isn't fear. I know what I'm afraid of: rats, tetanus, mold spores, high fructose corn syrup, pigeons. Whenever I watched movies with my friends I would opt to sit on the floor, or a chair of some type, but never the couch. I think that is why I got invited. My friends always rushed to the couch, they fought over it, but like Switzerland I stayed out of it. My grandpa taught me about Switzerland, always neutral, they kept their hands clean. I don't distrust couches; I'm not a crazy person. I even owned a couch, back in my apartment, but I used it more like a shelf, it was always full of life clutter while I made the effort to keep the rest of my apartment clean. I could sit, for example, on the breakfast bar. I sometimes perched there like a cat when no one was around. It might have been nice to get a cat, but I couldn't handle the fur all around, I'm not allergic I just don't like the messiness, or the smell of cat poop. Or the thought of it. Just poop laying around, just under a thin layer of sandy stuff that makes the cat feel better about itself, just no thank you.

The doorbell rang earlier. It seemed like the ring of a funeral bell. I'm not sure if it changed after I moved out or because of the person who rang.

Dad and Grandpa prepped that house, they found and rebuilt damaged solar arrays, attached two small wind turbines to the roof, even devised their own rain water filtration and had a good sized garden growing all before the big mess. Grandpa would say be prepared for anything. Even the yard had a 1.5 devron[24] tall fence around it, the windows made of bullet proof glass, rebar-reinforced concrete walls.

Chad seemed permanently aloof after his dad died. He often came over to my parent's place for dinner. I liked Chad, he was this link between me and my parents because when he was around it was easier to talk with them. He would show me the best movies from the far past that I wouldn't otherwise get to see. He collected them, often scavenging the city, because he loved the history and the stories they contained. His favorites? Into the Wild, Tideland, The Man Who Fell to Earth. When I answered the door, Chad was standing there in a slump. Mom invited him over, but he just wanted to talk with dad. Dad was a friend of Chad's father, so they

24. The only unit of planet-side distance measuring worthwhile, 1 devron is equal to approximately 2.1 meters or 6 feet and 9 inches.

could bond over him since he died when Chad was still a teenager. He called my dad Uncle Frank sometimes, but he called mom Iola even though she says he can just call her mom. We hung out for an hour before he left, right before dad got home from work, just the two of us. He asked when I got here and I told him I took the train last night, but I didn't tell him what happened with that beat-brain stalker.

Chad talked about a girl he met a few days ago, but she was strange and he was curious about her more than anything else. We chatted about how I like living alone for the first time and how work was going.

"Did you watch that documentary I gave you?"

It was CSM,[25] piecemeal and loose, a

Don't you know anything about modern advances in cinema?
The technique of crowd sourcing movies was soon to follow the
failed gimmicks of found footage and the reintroduction of
AromaRama in 2068. Crowd sourcing allowed for groups of
Refulgents to make films with smaller budgets and less work,
but since no new movies have been made in hundreds of years
people watch these poor excuses for entertainment as if they
were grandiloquent works of art. It started as a simple trend
of movies made by people from across the world, who've never
even met in many cases, using social networks. As the
popularity grew and these movies became monetized by
corporations, they became the focus of the media producing
industry due to their low cost and speed of production. A
craze in full swing by the time Iola was born. Of course,
technology did that thing technology does; gets smaller and
smaller until it lives within you mentally and physically.
People could watch movies any time they wanted. They could
even make a movie on the fly.
Yet even in the times before after-the-end there were issues.
Most issues were the result of the human mind's ability to
accept the images, only happening to few people with a
precondition for mental inflexibility. Combine that with the
failure to maintain the devices and their ability to be
passed down to a child in the womb, the devices themselves
believed inoperable after we came, some strange things began
happening in isolated cases. For instance, I dissected a boy
whose corpse was found in a pond. His mind's final act was to
record memories of his past on the date storage he was
unaware of even having. He was twelve when he drowned and
apparently was most interested in a small red three-wheeled
cycle device he rode regularly some six years earlier. The
red cycle's construction was poor quality and the boy's
stability was worse. Some other boys rode around a street
with maternal figures watching over them from nearby.
Is that a human thing? When I dissected several of my own kind
after the crash, many had final thoughts of the crash itself.
They had thoughts about how to survive and their minds
conjured images of what that survival might look like on a
new planet. My own mind had images of a great spire-tower
they'd build as an embassy to Earth in several generations.
Did we die thinking of the future while they die thinking of
the past? Is there any relevant psychological or sociological
information in that? I know my final thoughts, this new me,
will be of nothing at all. There is no imperative. Does it
imply anything about where we believe we'll go 'after'? The
great no-after. The known universe is merely a limitation to
overcome- with time it will expand and become known to
itself. Limitations are quelled with time.

documentary on Vishnu stated to be the creator of unlimited universes.

"The content was interesting. Not sure I understood it all, but I loved the art pieces they showed. Everything was sort of jarring how it was put together."

"I've never seen a CSM I liked," Chad said, "but I love the idea of it."

"You mean how people can put together something so big?"

"The pure passion it takes- these people are total stranger getting together over something they love. Is that even possible anymore?"

He continued talking like a man on a rushed walk without a particular destination. It's not that he liked the sound of his own voice so much as just investigating his own ideas aloud, and I loved being there to listen even if most of the time I'd just distracted by my own thoughts and delve into my own ideas. Chad knew it happened and would smile when he noticed how far apart our mind's drifted.

"I wouldn't want you listening to every

word I said anyway."

Chad's face dropped from a whimsical state to a serious, adult state.

"I wanted to wait for your dad to get here, but I'm just so excited," Chad restarted.

"What about?"

"I left the city the other day." Chad had a smile big enough to see from space.

"You left Boston? Why on earth would you do that?"

"Because I'd never done it before, and I've never know anyone who has. Do you?"

"No. No! Of course not."

"There is a lot out there, Liz, it's our future and our past. We can't just hide in the city forever."

"Nobody is hiding, this is where we live."

"We lived, spread across the world once. With machines to help us travel anywhere. A world of discovery."

"Machines and discovery that almost caused our extinction and the end of the world."

"We don't know that for certain. There is a lot we can learn, find."

"The city is safe, Chad, you don't know what's out there."

"I dunno what, exactly, I found a...a... zone where everything is..." his voice faded out.

"Like a daydream?" I asked. "Sounds like a movie."

"No, I'm serious. I couldn't stop wondering, you know, why the world changed. What was the purpose? I hiked out there," Chad continued.

"*Out there!?* That doesn't even make sense."

"I stumbled upon it, it is only about 19 k-devrons or so west of here. At Weeks Cemetery,[26] but the place has a pull. Logan has it partially cordoned off, they're cautious of entering."

"Whats there?"

"Creatures, maybe. Or something important from the old age!"

---

26. A cemetery once surrounded by state wildlife refuges and forests; long been my home.

"What are you even talking about? This is too much."

"There are places within the zone where gravity is at half its strength, and others where water will grab a hold of anything it touches, surrounding it like the wind, and burn it into oblivion. There isn't any thing alive out there. I didn't even see a squirrel or hear the chirp of a bird."

"It's been months since I've heard a bird, Chad."

"I spent three days walking around aimlessly until I needed to come back for supplies. It looked like a crash. Like a city crashed down from the sky."

"It's dangerous! Chad, this whole thing sounds crazy."

"No, I know, but it's real. It's something."

"*Something*? That's worth risking your life for?"

"I won't know until I go back."

"You can't!" I froze, I'd just blurted the words out. I had no intention to back them up with reasons, feelings, or understanding. It wasn't even that long ago, but I was so much younger then.

"I need to know, Liz. About the past, and whatever happened, even if there is nothing to find ever, I can't stop looking. If nothing else, I found a lot of usual... things, machine parts and artifacts, maybe. Trees are growing through the wreckage."

"You really plan on breaking into a Guard zone to salvage some junk and see trees? There is a reason we don't need trees anymore!"[27]

"Liz."

"I just don't see it.[28] You're choosing to leave us when you don't have to."

"I'm already 24, we won't be living as

27. Global warming caused exponentially growing fear well into the 2200s. The result of this fear was massive deforestation, because Refulgents in groups posses no logical capacity or reason. Luckily, as has been the case through all of known human history, a handful of intelligent people existed as well. Two of them created invisible-to-the-human-eye algae webs covering much of the Earth's oceans, in the atmosphere, and elsewhere that more than make up for the loss of nearly all plant life on the surface of the Earth.
28. Some people spend years of their lives in ignorance and bliss and pain until they emerge as one of the intelligent. Some people never make it that far, they tap out, they stop seeking, searching, yearning and believe the lies that pain, bliss, and ignorance project. Most people just find an excuse. The true sign of an intelligent species is its ability not just to accept change, but to desire and demand it.

long as our parents... I don't know how long we'll live without the treatments they had. I want to do something with my life before it's over without me knowing it."

* * *

His name is Guy, and I worked with him at the water dispensary. He thought this was a date. His parents aptly named him. He is not Chad, or Chad-like, but when I could I'd pretend he is. He doesn't know; nobody can see my thoughts. He had recently moved out on his own, too. Guy is messy; messy hair, messy clothes, dirt under his finger nails. We only came together out of some weak occupational connection and mutual disconsolance. I wasn't sure what the movie was because I couldn't stop worrying about the couch I was on with Guy. It was sucking me down to the depths of hell, maybe somewhere worse, and people generally find it weird if I keep moving to adjust, to escape, so I didn't move. He put his arm around my shoulders, but I had mixed feelings: happy because it meant he liked me, sad because it pushed me farther down into the couch, and worse my shirt had slid up held between me and the couch back exposing my skin to the horrific floral fabric, which was scratchy. I inwardly shuddered so he wouldn't think it was because of him.

It's not because I liked Guy, but I wanted him to like me.

I couldn't concentrate on this movie or on Guy at all. I had to fake being an adult in front of him to show him that I was strong, that I wouldn't be a burden to him, and to make certain for myself. I was scared of growing up; when it's real, when I could no longer pretend to be an adult or a child or anywhere in between at will.

I began to think that my skin was turning into the fabric of the couch, because of the scratching. Slowly my back turned blue with small white and pink flowers dotted across it, and it spread to my arms until my entire body was covered. I was becoming a me-couch-hybrid creature and nobody noticed. I was, as I'd folded down into a turtleish stature, a child couch.

What was my mission? What could I do with my
new life? Should I use these new powers to
scare people? Can I do something great now
that I was not a regular human, like show
everybody that humans are more similar than
different: "We are not so different" they
will say to each other while uniting to shun
me.

"Do you like the movie?" Guy asked
while he leaned in towards me, snapping my
mind back to reality, but I could hear him
just fine from where he was.

Pretending it was *Brazil*[29] I told Guy
that I liked it. It wasn't *Brazil*, but
Something and Someone are Dead and it seemed

---

29. A science-fictional film from the year 1985 B.T.E.[30] about
a retro-futuristic world and an oppressive totalitarian state
in which Robert DeNiro[31] plays a renegade air conditioning
repairman. Their odd estimations of the future were all
considerably incorrect from what I can tell, but interesting
none-the-less. Why does the air conditioning need repairmen?
30. While we are uncertain of the total number of years in
this period previously referred to as "A.D." we do know that
it has been about 200 years since "The End" as the nuclear
derived electromagnetic pulse event is commonly called, so
the period of years before this era are called "Before The
End" merely for dramatic effect.
31. POTUS 52, after the generally considered failed
presidency of a John Quincy Adams clone, President DeNiro
steered the country into a cultural golden age of
entertainment that restored the standard of living throughout
the 68 states. Their POTUS is much like our Grand-Zeal.
Centralized thinking for the greatest of good in an ever
darkening and dangerous world. What would we do without them.

good but I didn't want to like it and I wasn't in the mood for fate.

"We should do this more often."

"Do you usually watch movies like this?" I asked, grabbing for anything to say, but instead of answering he just kept leaning in towards my face... "I'm just glad it wasn't CSM." His face smelled like beeswax[32] and his breath was like baking soda and mint. I guess he wanted a kiss, a confirmation of a connection between us, but I wasn't there. As he got extremely close I had to fake a sneeze to keep my personal space, I had just returned to humanity after transforming into a couch creature and I needed to regain my personal bubble.

---

32 . Hypothetically speaking the mammal races of the earth are vermin, they can be extinguished with relative ease, however the bugs of this world are much further evolved in this sense and could survive much greater a calamity than even the Refulgents could. The usefulness of insects outweighs that of man, although many of their uses are in relation to the food chain. Refulgents eat the bugs, and in an accident of fate, animal milk was no longer readily available or widely remembered. Instead, almond milk was the norm, which generally speaking improved the health and wellbeing of the creatures who devour it.

Zero

My shift began the same, hum in
the dark with no escape, but the hum
rattles in your head even when we'd sleep
and I only
thought it was sleep. Except this time,
outside the ship, was a gaseous giant planet
that orbits the same
star as the Refulgent world we seek. The
Sapphire Jewel
sits outside the window now as I
write this letter, a whole new hum
here. It's hard to fully grasp what you have
accomplished by coming here, the quiet
sounds of rain
and thunder below us, and it is hard to
imagine
what I will accomplish when we meet the
creatures who live here.
The stasis process takes a quarter of
your planet's rotation to fully awaken
my subjects, perhaps this will be our last
letter home for
some time as we adjust to a new life; we
won't have

the time to write me a short letter, so a
long one will have to do.
The trip here was quite uneventful,
as we Zeals, and I, would no doubt prefer.
It has been a long time
since we left... You're not even sure who
this letter will be
sent to. My sister, dear ♪∂ʜ♭♫, you hope
they are well, or perhaps
we are long dead,
and my progeny receive this letter. Have you
told them
about me? About how you would sneak
out during the night to watch
the stars, how angry father would
get because of how tired I'd be
in the mornings, especially after mom died,
forced to do chores.
While I've been in stasis you had
dreams
of that time, you were young
and happy, most of the time, I didn't worry
about silly interstellar implications of
finding and meeting
alien life or how all society was on the
verge of
tearing myself apart.
Space travel, seeing worlds much larger
than ours,
and numerous, makes it all seem

— ∂ʜʜʔK

George's

Transient Downturn

Reality is reality whether it really happened or not. I walked out of the station because I was confused. How had I even gotten there? George: remember! The air smelled like sour milk and my head felt as if I'd been crying. Even if it's not a reality we've all shared, reality is in the mind of the beholder. Sometimes. I think. Reality is reality whether it really happened or not. Do we see the same view as others? Darkness backwards and lightness forwards, or as our hair and voices differ are the insides such amounts different? As I

measure the curve of the roadway I walk. How
do I measure the thoughts and the memories,
the feelings and the dispositions, the
matter and dismatter in the other than I?
Some are like waves, but can be predicted
easily while others are like the night sky
with endless amazement. Is your reality the
same as mine or is that the point?

My emotional state rebounded as I
jaunted down the station's stairs into the
city, trying to whistle the songs I've heard
from birds throughout my life, trying to
calm myself and blend into the coming dawn.

I had thought everything was getting
better.

Saraswati sent me on an expedition to
find her friend. She said we could share his
friendship, a perennial somewhere south of
I-90. He is said, said Saraswati, to be one
of the wisest, most powerful in all the
world- the ancient Ganesha. I was to find
him inside a large obsidian colored cube
between the city and the sea with history
inside.

Crossing the boarder of I-90. Returning

one again to the apocalypse of ancient decay
I was immediately sad by the state of
absolute abandon. Everything was red with
neglected, alone, it hurt to walk through
with no way to offer change.

Buildings are meant to be lived in.

I heard a roar from the havoc of what
was once apartments and suddenly a beast the
size of a dozen dogs leaped from the iron
scraps. The beast chewed on iron rust from
the collapsed ancient carapace. Mid-
mastication it looked up and noticed me. The
beast roared and I ran while wetting my
pants. The apples Saraswati sent with me
tumbled to the ground. The beast crushed
them with hoofed feet and so much force they
burst like the explosives they used in the
old world; magnalium mixed with strontium,
potassium perchlorate,[33] and... and... what
else? Fire burst as the stomp of the beast

---

33. Flowers bursting out from a single point explosion
launched high in the sky; once a symbol of the country
chemistry was an important step in human understanding. It is
quite amazing how they've lost most science, in that it is
not taught but imprisoned in books long forgotten, yet
religion has suffered the same fate. It will be interesting
to see where they land as more of them have no knowledge or
nostalgic stories of the previous Earth.

exploded the skin of the apple in all directions.

I fled through an iron curtain of rusted mist that seemed to emanate from the back of the beast; I ran as fast as I could.

The beast followed.

I ran.

I could *feel* the monster, heavy gravity was all around me, come hot and powerful and ancient, like a rocket piercing through the sound barrier, that wrecked clouds and mountains alike. The beast was not from this world- it devoured it, showing me true destruction up close and in progress. The quadruped forced itself towards me with destruction meant to stop flowers from blooming, children from dreaming, life from living. Mist flowed off its back like a cape dissipating towards the horizon.

The monster was anti-love with a sly, indicating smile.

Passing through a thicket I entered a glen, a hole of peace somehow placed between the corpse-shells of buildings on all sides, and music[34] was playing. The glen was accompanied by several plastic climbing tubes that children once played on surrounding a dinner table. The music seemed to emanate from every direction.

"Hello, friend, don't mind me." A small human-like creature hummed.

"I'm... I'm..."

"Running, I know. Covered in sweat. Out of breath. Lost your apples?"

"My apples... I need those... where are we?"

"This place is mine. Nobody enters here without my knowing, my approval. I saw you chased by that horrible beast, I helped you." All at once: completely weasel, man, horse, tiger, dragon, and woman. The only thing in common between the creature's shifting forms was a spider-like movement and deep red paint covering its body like clothing.

"Thank you."

"You are my guest. Have a seat," it

---

34. Light strong strings played with discord and plenty of sinister factor playing against tubas, oboes, and French horns playing "Dire Wolf" by the Greateful Dead.

said pointing to the table made of ancient wood surrounded by chairs uncomfortably close together, none matching, with a smattering of chipped, broken, and pulverized vitreous, translucent ceramic material resembling the shell of a cowrie spread across the surface.

"Won't the beast follow?"

"No." It said while running fingers through porcelain dust.

"How can you be sure?"

"I can be, yes. Absolutely certain. Those monsters have no food here."

I slowly wandered a few paces while gazing around, "aren't we his food?"

"Oh no, no, no. Of course not. They eat the ruin." It's stature was amorphous as it pulled a human corpse out of a plastic tube and brought it to the table, posing it in a seat. I felt as if I must've been dreaming, but I knew I was awake.

"Why did that thing chase me?"

"To kill you. You startled it. Perhaps it thought you were hunting him. Creatures, they have instincts," it hoisted another corpse from another tube, sitting it in another chair.

"It was never this dangerous before."

"Well, it isn't "before" now, is it?"

This creature did not seem dangerous, but when I saw how he handled the corpse with ease and whimsy I knew he could be malignant. He was some kind of powerful hermit beat-brain or beat-brain god.

"What is your name?"

I told him my name, he told me he has had many names since the start, "I am from and of the earth. I come from far out," but I could call him Iktomi; Iktomi was male, or the creature's all-at-once-ness disguise had given up, or decided, and presented me with one solid and consistent image. A tall, hunched man, only slightly older than myself, with brown hair like mine reaching down below his knees. "It is all rather simple if you can see all of human time. You won't have to worry about any of that for awhile yet. Maybe you'll be ready in the future. I'm not sure. I'm really rather uncertain. Good luck. You, well, you I like."

"What are you preparing for?" I asked knowing all along he saw nothing wrong or strange with how he handled the bodies, that if I offended him I might become one- a prop- and that his power so exceeded my own that once I entered the glen with Iktomi I would never be in control again.

Iktomi was more interested in cleaning dishes with his button-less, open sleeve, then he muttered: "When there are clouds in the sky, and they are all brown, always brown, you may be sad, but remember they'll soon pace away."

"Okay..."

"Look-" he gestured around the glen, "do you see the point?"

"What is the point?"

"-not everything has a point. For example, a pencil is pointless."

"A what?"

"Never mind, well, I want to know a ploy to distract us- There are apples, right there, on that tree."

On the table appeared a whittled

porcelain tree with the largest apples I'd
ever seen almost crying off the branches.
Twice the size of the ones Saraswati grew,
the apples were dark red and every shade
till light yellows emerged. I quickly began
to devour one from each hand.

"Yesterday was the perfect day to be
lonely," Iktomi started, "but today it seems
companionship is in order. This transient
form is nothing more than a nodule. You are
only a piece of what you think of as
'self.'"

I ate.

"Each 'individual' is nothing more than
a non-periodic signal, a decaying signal, we
are but an effect produced outside of the
mind."

Apple after apple, it felt like a
trance as I focused on Iktomi's words.

"We are on a journey, an experience, to
new realms of thought. The scope and content
of the experience is limitless."

As I ate I felt strange.

"Turn on! Think for yourself."

All of a sudden my entire

waking life
seemed to be a dream,
then a terror,
then not mine
I was laughing and crying in turn about
it all, then moving on, instant after
instant a new life.
I felt as if my body was filled with
air instead of blood, like I could float and
if I tried to hum I would, I could, but I
didn't.
I tried to stay on the ground,
the moment passed like
ripples *across* a pond
I got scared I missed it forever-
cursed to walk the land as I always
had, blood bodied. I felt like all of life
is some kind of careful balance between
holding back
letting loose
just enough
to keep from destroying
butterfly wings with dragon's fire
until only few truths remain.
The look and feel of porcelain had

become miraculous to me. The dust ran through my fingers, *my* fingers, I could see the origin of life, I was the source of the Earth and sun and every moon there was! I was a rising wave! I was-

Wait, no. Is that right? Wait.

I felt sick. Unsure. Where exactly was I?

"I'm alive now, right now; confirmed now. For now." Iktomi looked at me with a smirk.

My lungs were rebuilt by butterflies which is why I *can* fly and my brain used to be mush but Saraswati helped me repair it- the lightening struck the lump of clay and it was alive. A brain built of brains, each growing on top of the previous until a usable whole was formed.

A trail of turtles, 17 long, limbs of fire and shells of ice, crossed my path. The second 7th turtle grew large as a carriage when the line stopped in front of me so I hopped on his back and went for a ride. The turtle's back elongated as he turned into a dragon, long and thin, with a mane of unburning fire. The dragon tried to fly, but its weight kept us down and its paws created chasmic prints.

The rest of the turtles cried as their brother screamed from growth then began collapsing in on himself like an imploding star, slowing the passage of time until nothing moved at all. I smiled at the wonder until I was amazed to see Saraswati gracefully, yet powerfully, grow from the ground before me.

"Hold. You have stumbled into a rare and pivotal moment," is how she greeted me.

When her words stopped, on that exact beat, Iktomi dropped from Saraswati's branches with a charming smile and a nasal exertion of triumph.

"We've met, you'll remember me for sure- from the past if I'm not mistaken." Iktomi spouted with uncertain sincerity. "You may not know this guy though."

A long, white haired man dressed in magnificent robes that looked as midnight does with a pale lunar glow and galactic twinkling stood on the other side of

Saraswati as if he'd been there even a
moment earlier.

"The races of earth..." he started.

"Groovy, I guess Yeomy is going first,"
Iktomi forced in.

"Have fallen. The earth itself
survives. Life survived. Power has dominion
now, the beasts and men have been reduced in
so great a number that any can take command!
Those who want will win." Yeomra finished.
He spoke with force, like he'd practiced the
lines a thousand times before.

"You humans, finally, have fallen, like
me, but you are only *just*, so young, so
barely even there. I have lasted since
perhaps the very moment that lasting
started. Only, on that day not long ago when
I witnessed your landing hard did I begin to
notice, reflect on my befallen state. Like
an addict or a fool I refused to realize the
waste of it all..." Iktomi trailed off as he
stared at the ground.

In the dead air Yeomra started again:
"Some die and that's it, they're done-
others though, with no great power or

ability, can become so much more. I lied, mind you, it takes the greatest power of all- sheer will. Not the will to live or to be great, but the will to expand and learn; to become wholly self and individual gives us the discretion to make greatness as we please."

Saraswati took control once Yeomra finished. "George, please follow along. You know you can if you focus. Don't force it, allow it to enter your mind, but do not allow it to take over- entertain the ideas as you did when we have spoken in the past. Wait until they finish speaking each, then take your time to review what they told you. Decide on your own time." Iktomi performed a small leap of joy as Saraswati finished.

"Decide when you will, as long as you decide on me! But, listen now: The powerful always have followers, if they seek to or not, and not because they need followers but because the followers need them. Coyote follows me. The bulgasari follow Yeomra. Saraswati follows Ganesha.

Those who want power always seek

followers, demand them in some cases, but that is a weak zardozian power, an authority not earned or achieved through valid means. In the end though, power is a means to the oft forgot end. Both are likely meaningless.

The search- for power or anything else, anything at all- is infinite and important." Iktomi made in-place dances as he seemed to lose interest in his own words.

"Once, the populations of creatures expanding across the world outnumbered the power and abilities of the gods, but no more and never again! The bulgasari will keep this world free." Yeomra enjoyed his own words as much as he expected me to.

"We must create new life. Like none we've seen before, creatively, but sill, however, we only have the parts and supplies from what we can find already invented. Pretty hard. I've been working on it for a while, considerable intellect up here, but nothing groovy yet... just a matter of time." Iktomi's tone continued and he seemed more and more to just be thinking out loud. I could tell he was afraid of Yeomra- and I was afraid of him.

Still trapped in icebound time, the mane of fire I'd been grasping off the back of a brand new dragon whelp shocked me when I remembered it was there upon glancing down; distracted by the mesmerizing conversation before me. What could I have done to possibly deserve this?

"George. Now do you realize some new ideas? Take control of time as needed." Saraswati said.

"Well, wow," then I paused; when I came back I felt as though I had an answer: "You are both coeval, opportunistic, and shallow; in any other world you'd belong together in prison. Saraswati is the only one I would follow, and she would not use me for her own ends or glory. I'm uncertain of reality, but for now I am exhausted of this."

Yeomra vanished before another word, but Iktomi was quick to say: "You may feel you've chosen wisely- but by the time you slowly die before your family deep beneath the dirt, and time once again trickles to a stop for you, you will regret."

Saraswati's branches swayed in the breeze, as if to smile, then she returned into the ground. The icy flow of time began to mollify.

The turtle-dragon's final act was to eject me from his back, launching me through the apple scented air and just for a second my sight went black.

Before I knew it I was back outside the glen, alone, much later in the day, with no trace of Iktomi, but I could still hear his voice.

"Ice baker. Lemon squeezer. Hydrant kicker. Son of twenty beers. Tomorrow pointer."

I looked around for the glen, for Iktomi, for a trace of what I should be doing, but instead I found myself laughing aggressively and alone, accompanied only by mist.

"I'm bored. I'm board. I'm a board. I'm aboard. I'm starboard. Wet and cold. Floating. I'm shrinking. Midnight running." Iktomi's voice continued to float around, "What's the frequency?"

That anti-love beast sprung back into view. It had been waiting; knowing I would return; knowing there would be no joy in letting me live; knowing there would be glory in my pain. Built like a lion and the size of a bear, the bulgasari are monstrous beasts that destroy with violent ease, explosive movements, and terrifying glee. The beast had weight as it careened through rusted down garbage dumpsters that had formed an accidental wall with ease and, perhaps, to show me how *nothing* I was before it. Teeth; dozens of mismatched, chunky, nasty teeth; some broad and dull others sharp and peaked, but the look in its eye made it a terror: a green electric glow from inside its pupil that chortled like a hundred children lost in the dark. Glowing green blazed in lighting-like lines tattooed over the monster's back and along its ribs. Its head was mostly mouth, a powerful jaw; the rest of it was muscle with eight inch torn-metal-like jagged claws tearing forth off five seven-digit paws.

I tripped.

Last I heard from Iktomi was: "George?" said in a long, flat tone that echoes the halls of the deepest darkest backward of my mind to this moment.

Then I fell onto bright pink and yellow blooms looking up at two men with skin as brown as the sky, clothes like none I'd seen before, and strange qualities to their voices- who appeared seemingly out of nowhere. We'd vanished from where I was to somewhere nearby. The first man had a tuxedo suit that was so clean he seemed to be from another dream and the whites of his teeth sparkled with astral beauty.

"My name is Dinesh, do not be afraid." His speech was both calm and aware, "you are in danger here, Sir, but Gangrim and I have come to help."

The other man, more brutish, wore leather lamellar armor and bracers that had been chewed on by large creatures.

"Bulgasari," Gangrim said.

Gangrim revealed a large, seven-branched sword he called Chiljido that was made of crystal or something of equal wonder. The blade itself was wet with fresh blood, Gangrim carried that smell deep within himself as if forever marked by the battles he has fought.

"I've been fighting Bulgasari since the aliens came. Dinesh will take you someplace safe until our friend arrives." Gangrim then left with the speed of a shooting star to fight the beast.

Dinesh's grace, a pure adroitness, whisked us from the imminent danger of the beast and the molder of South Boston, south and into the water. Not into, but onto. Dinesh held us afloat as if we could stand on the water surface by his sheer power of will.

"The old harbor," he said, "it was nice here this morning."

"What, what was that? How did you...?"

The force of the blows between Gangrim and the beast caused the sea to wave at the sky with jealousy.

"A mind divided against itself will surely fall, George. The lysergic acid doesn't help."

"Lie... sir...?"

"Never mind. It's in those apples, most foul, where did you receive them?"

"I got after I left Saraswati. I broke the ones she gave me."

"Saraswati sent you?"

"We are friends. I felt bad about breaking her apples, so I was happy when Iktomi offered to give me more."

"These are impure. Fundamentally dirty. Can you not tell the difference?"

"I do... feel..." I gazed into the remainder of an apple in my left hand.

"It is a feeling like these waves- some strong, others insane, but they all repeat and feel like different lives- You must not worry. All will pass, if you allow it it will pass smoothly."

"Where are we?"

"Haha. No worries my friend. We are safe here."

"Yeah. This is nuts, man."

"As anything else, it is nothing more than a ride. The ride will end and you will only remember the parts you want to remember."

"Yeah. Yeah. Okay. Okay. Clouds fill the sky, but, you know, they'll soon go away."

"Wise words, my friend. Just keep waiting here with me a little longer. Gangrim called a friend of ours to take you home."

An almost golden haired monkey arrived on a small, floating cloud. Dinesh lifted me with one arm onto the cloud; it was neither passable nor impassable, yet warm and fluffy. I instantly felt drowsy.

Gangrim rejoined me, "Haeng un." Dinesh dashed to fight the bulgasari.

"Hang on?"

"It means good luck."

"I'm trying to go over there," I yawned, pointing to a large black cube across the bay.

Half looking, Gangrim said "You cannot."

"Why?"

"Your true journey lies not here. Join this monkey on his journey, he owes us this labor."

"Then where am I supposed to go now?"

"A wise man once said: Take the world in a love embrace, fire all of your guns at once and explode into space." For only a moment I closed my eyes.

The next instant I awoke next to the golden haired monkey in time to watch the cloud disperse into vapor wisps. The monkey seemed to smile and nod. I stood up, but the wind was strong and the rust flecks scratched my skin as they whirred about the city air.

Zero

The falling gyre that transfigured the Earth changed us too.

You thought we were crazy.

You thought we were alone.

A universe empty to us.

When we understood differently, you refused to. You tried to explain away the transmissions, but once we heard them, once we saw those alien images, once our planet was reduced and forced to reform, anarchy! A divide that became one sided and soon the *ones* like me had to make a decision. The many chose to ignore and live with ignorance in their hearts. We few chose differently. We chose to seek. We knew things would fall apart.

It took two secluded decades for us to build the ships. Ten times four million of us could have come, but we could not find enough willing to explore: the first alien species and us without wonder. The creature's transmissions show us their lives, their location, and their love of Lucy.

We had no way of communicating with them prior to our arrival. We had no way of predicting their mentality, their acceptance, their understanding. The Earth was far less ready than we. Knowing there was more out there, among the stars, would change them, we only wanted to learn about them, to help temper the attitudes of isolationism and broaden the narrow views on both sides.

We failed.

— Zeal Prime

49.5 Part 2 – Elizabeth

For some reason I was having trouble jumping on a trampoline for six hours in nothing but this cute red and yellow two-piece. I had only seen clothes like that in old magazines and photographs that were faded brown. It could have been longer, the jumping. At apogee I could see car races over the fence, but otherwise I was only surrounded by warm oceanic air. It was so nice, or it would have been if my legs weren't burning from their constant exertions. The sky was blue like in paintings. I don't know why I didn't stop bouncing, especially as I began to sweat so much that it soaked the once strawberry red

of my swimsuit into a more rosewood color
that I wasn't in the mood for since it grew
dark, almost blood-like. The sweat glistened
off my skin, which was gross, I couldn't
help but want to shower, and even though I
wasn't sticky from sweat yet I knew that was
coming and I was already uncomfortable. It
was nice to see a blue sky- I'd never seen
that before. It was nice to see a yellow,
soft sun- never seen that either. For once
the chirps birds sounded melodic instead of
frantic, clawing. It really was so nice, for
a time.

My belly growled as if in extreme
hunger and from my mouth sprung the squeal
of a rhino. All my body fat collapsed in on
itself and I became a flesh skeleton, but as
I did a back-flip the fat came back and
more, my stomach distended like a pregnancy.
I could feel my back and breasts ache. I
coughed up blood. A stillborn fetus
jettisoned out of me, bouncing with me while
I wished it had lived at least as much as
me.

I returned to normal. I decided to

focus on the sweat droplets as they flew off my body with each bounce into the open sky, through space and time, delving through long uncut blades of grass to splatter on fresh dirt.

Real children require attention and care, all the time. You can't even blink or they will get into something. In dreams they are an external expression of your inner change, or vulnerability, I had read. Dreams can be anything, can't they, so why couldn't I dream something new each night? Why did I have to feel alone when surrounded by people.

There was something bothering me about everything biological, but I chose not to think about it. I didn't want to think about that baby. I chose to be distracted.

Chad had been missing for over a week. Eleven days. Dad didn't utter an indication of his thoughts, but I knew he was thinking Chad jumped. I knew Chad would never, could never, I don't know why, I just knew, but jumping was the easiest thing to believe, wasn't it? Because: Do people love only

eating bread and water in between dwindling
supplies of nutra-meals? Because: Do people
enjoy every day brown skies and every night
enforced curfew, no running water, minimal
electricity rations, and crazy radiation
addled minds doing whatever they please? The
worlds we'd seen in art and movies had much
more ingrained possibility than ours. Things
seemed bleak on the best days. That's why it
was easy for anyone to believe Chad had
jumped.

I'd stolen my father's torch.[35] He had
other weapons, several in fact, so he
wouldn't miss this one. I figured the torch
had the most utility. I knew exactly where
Chad had gone, Weeks Cemetery. I knew of the
graveyard since the family wanted to bury
Grandpa at Weeks, but of course couldn't.

I was half way there before realizing
how mindlessly I'd rushed after Chad,
selfishly, on this stolen, dirty, mud coated
bike. The back tire wasn't inflated

---

35. This particular Torch could launch 45 miniature flare-
bullets in 9.6 seconds in rapid fire mode. Each bullet burns
at 2251 degrees Fahrenheit and could melt anything from a
book to a man.

properly, the handle-basket kept my gun from falling and after a few hurried miles I stopped caring how dirty the contraption was. I brought no food, just my thoughts of food once my belly began to rumble. I brought no shelter, which somehow made me miss my apartment and the thought of camping out made me even miss the couch.

I envisioned my old people sitting in their Jesus room with a modest fire lit, holding each other close on that chilly evening, discussing their favorite passages from Psalms and thanking each other kindly for their input. I imagined they had individual favorite lines, had them embroidered on pillows, but they accepted each other without a wavering thought or feeling.

I imagined some brat playing my Yoshi's Island, but when I realized they didn't have a way to recharge the battery; I felt bad for them. I wondered about what kind of person they were: boy or girl, nice or mean, good or bad.

I realized a growing rumble within me

and tried to ignore it. I realized I didn't know what I was doing and that I couldn't admit to myself why I was doing it.

My head ached, and I grew more and more irritable about everything. I wanted my Yoshi's Island back, and Chad; why did you have to disappear when you could have stayed home? You could have been safe and warm at your place or mine. There was no need for you or I to have gone out to the unknown. I regretted it all. Why couldn't we have been honest? Why couldn't everything just be wonderful, and simple, and easy, and mine?

I needed to concentrate on my task, but I couldn't; all I had were scatter brained imaginings that got blurrier and blurrier the more I looked into them.

It took me over six hours of imaginings and realizings until I got to that damn cemetery. Forever and not long at all, which made me realize the danger of the situation and that I shouldn't be day dreaming there; I hadn't noticed my follower at all.

"Are we there yet?" He asked in a friendly, natural way.

I almost shot him, in the face, but-
click click- the safety was on.

"Get away from me!" I demanded, and
flipped to red.[36] Even beat-brains know what
that means. "Don't get any closer!" Had he
been following me since the train?

"I brought you apples," he said while
holding out a bucket full of strangely
shaped red things the size of small fists
that looked as if they belonged next to a
ginger jar in fiction.[37] My stomach was
audible. I was on the verge of passing out.

"You followed me to give me that?"

"Saraswati gave me them to share with
you. She told me you were here and would
need help."

"This is food?" I knew I shouldn't
easily trust my stalker and attacker. Did I

---

36. Red has various connotations to the people of this land:
fire, risk, death, courage, and passion. I think, weirdly,
that Liz meant some combination of all these and more.
37. Vincent van Gogh's still life with ginger jar and apples,
long mistakenly thought to be a representation of a fictional
foodstuff before the rediscovery of "fruit" as historical
fact. Also, if you recall, the source behind the alternate
title of the first log. You know, now that I think about it,
it has been several decades- maybe more- since our last
contact. This transmission may reach you in transit to my
location, or may reach a dead planet, best to believe you are
on the way. This solar system is the future of the Lebagir.

have it in me to kill him if I needed to?

"Totally natural, and clean, and present."

I was hungry. I'd never seen a real red food, can you imagine, eating red food?

His extended arm place an apple before my eyes as I collapsed to the ground with a huff.

"I don't want anything from you. Keep back." I limply held the torch pointed in his general direction- it's hard to miss with a torch. The creeper sneaked behind me and helped me sit up. My eyes only closed for a moment, I swear. The torch dropped to the dust and before I knew it I was chewing the flesh of a bright red apple. I swallowed that apple meat, it shocked me conscious, I knew it was a mistake but I was lucky and the food was good. What was I thinking?

It was delicious, like nothing I had ever tasted, and the inside was fairly and comfortably brown. I knew I shouldn't have taken it, not from him, but I couldn't hold out; it looked clean, he wasn't lying about that, it was crisp and fresh like nothing

I'd ever eaten.

"This food has water in it?" I asked him.

"Nature knows what it's doing."

"I'm not comfortable with you here, with you following me." I stood up and paced.

"I've brought more food."

"How the hell did you follow me?" I knew I needed his food.

"Transportation is a good way to get around." He displayed a small, children's bicycle. He smiled kindly despite his well-worn face.

"What or who is Saraswati?! How did you know I would be here?" Perhaps you can imagine my frantic, confused tone.

"Saraswati is my friend. She said you were here. She knows many things."

"Why did she tell you to come?"

"To help. I just have food." He lifted the bucket again, maybe 25... apples.

"That's a start... but you didn't answer my question."

"Worried. It gets really sunny out

here, away from the city, it gets fresh."

"Are you stalking me or what?" I
blurted.

"I wanted to apologize. In the subway.
Nothing happened."

"Nothing happened... I know," I calmed
down and knew my only advantage was to keep
control of myself.

"I was just confused then and you look
familiar. I was going to have a sister once,
but she didn't have a fat belly... she
wouldn't have."

"I do not have a fat belly!" I was
scared, not thinking, everything went so
fast, and I just reacted. I thought he was
trying to attack me, on the train, wasn't
he?

Beat-brains are known for their frailty
with communication and understanding of
social situations. Their brains are
basically rotting, betraying them. I
wondered if my initial impression of him was
wrong?

"But, not skinny either."

"You're a jerk," I mocked, "but since

you have more of those abbles I may be able to stand you for a little while." I realized he reminded me of Grandpa.

"Aren't you afraid?"

"Yeah, sort of." It would be better not to go it alone, Chad mentioned there were many dangers ahead. What if Chad is hurt and I need help rescuing him; my mind couldn't help but worry only about him.

"I mean the trucks, they growl and roar, never quiet, full of bees."

"You mean those troopers?"

"They're the old Coast Guardsmen. They work with the city buy are always outside of it. Can smell 'em from here."

"What's your name?"

"George the 3rd king of the brown and wearer of hats."

"Could I call you just George?"

"Or, just George it is."

"Whatever, we're losing daylight."

"Let's go." George started to move, but I had to be sure I could trust him. I had to try to know him. I trailed behind him to keep him in view.

"What's your favorite movie?"

"Movie?"

"Yeah. Haven't you seen any?"

"Never. You?"

"The Coastguard doesn't scare me since they won't be catching me," because I thought I had nothing else, "and I've never seem you wear a hat."

"Are movies any good?"

Chad was right, on some level, we won't be living as long as our parents were able to. There will be only so much time we have and I have no idea how much that is. I had to find Chad. No matter what. I knew he was all I had, and I love him.

* * *

I just didn't want to be alone. It had taken a while for the danger to dawn on me. I had no idea where Chad was, he could have been in a jail... or a grave. I didn't think George would do anything to hurt me, and I couldn't pull off whatever vague plan I'd devised that would help me save Chad without some help. Or maybe he was at home eating dinner with mom and dad laughing about how he'd tricked me into leaving the city. I rarely ventured out of my routine, but I was already acting inconsistently and I was sick of resenting the world. George, at least, had two more eyes to help me search.

I knew George was okay when we saw monkeys dancing across these ropes that hung between the carved trees that lined the road. George pointed- "he's their king" he said.

"How do you know?"

"I've met him before."

"Oh?"

"And he's got the best dance moves." George did some sort of off balance jig and spin.

"Where do you think they're going?"

"Some nice place."

"How do you suppose that?"

"Hope," he replied while tossing up apples to our merry monkey companions.

We got to the zone easily.

We overheard the Guardsmen.

"The walkies aren't working again, Sir. I sent Stephan to Ghiloni and Sebastien to

Charter Oak."

The one in charge had a large gun and a
small one at his hip. The one who spoke
looked as if he hadn't slept and held his
gun like it might try to escape. All of them
held their guns that way, with trepidation
like they spent sleepless nights surrounded
in the dark by the roars of monsters they
never saw. Something made the air dense. We
observed them for an hour and could tell
they were scrambling all over the place.
They sent runners to relay messages. I could
tell they were afraid. There was a distinct
border, a threshold, as distinct as walking
through a waterfall except it was not
something you could see. It was a feeling,
in the air, molecularly, that was obtrusive.
An unavoidable shutter was forced from our
bodies when we passed through it. The troops
never touched it, out of a fear that was
right. Once the jarring transition was over
we were in the past; the future of some
childish hopes; an alternate reality where
the world had colors and time was visible,
but meant nothing. The sky was peculiar, it

hued blue and everything was orchidaceous. I felt like Elanor without the picket fence,[38] and the whole place looked oddly like The Pool at Medfield[39] except it had a blight long derelict. Almost none of it was brown.

Covering the ground were tiny green spikes that smelled like those chemical packs we used to get to make a room smell better, yet they were soft and exuberant. Under the sunny blue sky the world looked alien. Trees, they're called, but I had never seen one in person before; they seemed alive almost willing to speak. I wished the world was covered in that soft green so that I could curl up and take a nap and sleep forever becoming something that belonged and was a part of this world. Throughout the

---

38. Frank Weston Benson; had the impression he was American like twenty five hundred years ago or whatever. His marble statue is all blotchy though; painter of Elanor on a picket fence.

39. *"Don't think, as they do, that the charm of an artist's work must be found also in his own personality. It is always apart, or should be, should have nothing to do with it, and that is what makes it such an infernal trade. Never to play on one's own twopenny flute but to keep the big end in view always; to remain patient and cold and quiet and work like a dog from morning 'til night; there is no other way of arriving even at talent, unless one is cut out of larger stuff than I am."* Dennis Miller Bunker, painter of the Pool at Medfield.

verdure was Chad's mystery, a million clumps
and clusters of metal all broken long ago;
some big and some small. In the distance I
could see large chamber sized discards of
some neglected construct.

It was easy to tell the time by the
light of the vault. The bright blueness of
the sky developed a gradient leading to
black; a strong night with another new
sight: stars. I had seen the likeness of
stars before, but no painting could contend
with the magnificence of that milky scar. I
could hardly believe it. It was like a
dream, the colors and shapes from every iris
I'd ever seen. In the city I could look out
and up barely catching a sense of what might
be there, a single dull twinkle in the
northern sky. An unearthly power, those
stars in the livid night sky, beyond wonder
into sheer magic. It seemed unreal. I fell
over as I strained my neck back as far as
possible, then farther.

I felt small. Is the out-there the same
as here? Could people go there? Are people
up there now, disconnected from us? Is such

a stupendous sight above me at all times and only now I have been made aware? How could anything I do matter with all that above me?

I wanted to run- but to where? It was all encompassing and great. If we'd known about this all humanity would gather here and tell stories and watch the sky like it's a drug that keeps us living.

We found a damaged, rotted wood shed and decided to set up for the night near it, but as we got close George began to giggle. Cautious of him, I stopped advancing, my hand immediately sought the torch in my waist band, but he was smiling and laughing to himself and when I finally saw him and questioned what he was so happy about he jumped into the air. He got about 2 devrons up before gently gliding back down.

"Groovy!" George shouted gleefully as he landed.

"Be careful, Chad told me about the weird things that happen around here. Also, beware of water."[40]

　　"What's wrong with it?"

　　"Chad said it will burn you worse than fire."

　　"Fire-water? Opposites do attract."

　　The place was completely unnatural. Water that burns you. Sky that doesn't push you down; a sky that isn't brown! It was a wrong place and the longer I suffered it the more I wanted to flee- but couldn't. I don't know why, I loved and always wanted what I saw there, but maybe it was too beautiful; my mind wanted to reject the idea of a place like that even being possible. It made my entire past hurt so much more.

　　Those stars, are they ours? No human could withstand them. If we could all see the night sky that I saw no work, or sleep, or religion would survive the encounter.

　　We decided the shed unsafe, so we trekked on for another hour to be sure and because we really didn't know what we were

---

40. It may be clear as an autumn lake, which is a body of various quantities of dihydrogen-oxide, but there is no water in the substance we call עשמ. The nearest substance I've found on earth might be jet fuel.

doing.

We found a different place to camp for the night, all dirt spots on the ground, but it got dark and eventually we needed to sleep; I knew that dirt would be part of the process. I was trying to accept it, for Chad's sake. The torch, single shot, was enough to light a fire from wood George had collected. The white-blue flare popped down the barrel in an all-out sprint for inevitably futile survival. The logs were wet, but the ember had little trouble igniting a bonfire that would warm us until morning.

"What's with your hair?"

"What?"

"You need a haircut."

"I cut it myself." George seemed proud and beamed a smile at me.

"It looks like it," I smirked.

Running his dirt caked finger tips through matted hair, George seemed self-conscious for the first time. "You don't like it?"

"Maybe it could use a comb."

"Where would I get one?"

"You don't have a comb?"

"No. Are they expensive?"

"They are not." I struggled not to laugh. "You can find one almost anywhere. We'll look for one on the way back into the city."

"Thanks!"

"You are kind. Just like Saraswati said you'd be. I'm glad we are friends now, because I was beginning to..."

I must have fallen asleep.

Not for any good reason, but it was a deep sleep that seemed to have taken longer than it did. I had the kind of dream you realize was a dream only after waking up. They weren't cats;[41] dozens of quarter devron long creatures with two-tails and violet eyes, long hair of varied grays with deep purple streaks. They'd dash around only in my peripherals while the giant fans that made up the six walls cut beams of outside artificial light and made maelstroms of

---

41. Felis catus, monsters in their own right and cuter than any other.

loose fur. In unison they hummed mis-
matching melodies[42] unfamiliar to me.

I stood in that single room like a
weeping angel covering my face from the fur.
After hours I picked up on their tunes and
hummed along, like a password the little
monsters jolted in place forming six rows of
six in a semi-circle before me. In creepy
fan chopped voices they, still in unison,
spoke: "We are the keepers of your inner
mind. You've never had a dream like this
before. We know this because your mind has
been our home ever since we finished
learning magic from our uncles."

"What are we doing here?" I asked them.

"Now is the winter of our discontent!
This you know!"

"You don't all have the same uncle?"

"No...what?"

"You implied you have different uncles,
not a shared uncle. Do you all have magical
uncles or something?"

"Well, you know, this is a complex

---

42. Two songs they seemed to mimic from the real world; I
could only tell by comparing the notes I had on file; Rainy
Day Women #12 & 35 by Bob Dylan and Swan Lake by Tchaikovsky.

situation. We can't just tell you everything, and our past is subject to varied and inconsistent retcon."

"If that's your idea of an answer..."

"We do that sometimes, sorry. Not a lot of conversation happening around here and its not like you have many friends."

"I haven't much need."

"Not since the baby."

"What is that supposed to mean?"

"Not your first loss, won't be your last. The world is complex and that's barely an answer. Surely by now you realize that real, meaningful answers are not given but uncovered and reflected on. You generate the truth for yourself."

"That sounds wonderful. So, anything I want can be real?"

"No. Truth has little to do with reality. Humanity always chooses that. There are no dreams, no honor remains, just the mind and what it makes of things. The arrow has left the bow long ago."

"Where is the arrow now?"

"Hard to say."

"What then?"

"Become the dew that quenches the land."

"I think I hate it here..."

"Then leave. You are always free to leave. It is your mind after all."

"How can I leave?"

"Laugh."

"That's it? Laugh?"

"You would have guessed so eventually. What did you think you'd have to do, tap your heels?"

In the morning I found that our campsite was next to somebody's former respite. I figured it had to have been Chad's. I knew he'd gone out here, alone, looking for mysteries, looking for meaning, or whatever he could find, I knew he hadn't jumped. All I had to do was figure out which way he'd gone and follow the trail.

But like a sponge gently placed on a puddle, slowly soaking the loose water into its pores, 'not since the baby' seeped back into my mind and my memories began to congeal together in one place. "Not since the baby" meant something to me. How could I be certain of anything if I could so easily undo my own past. How could you confirm something as intangible as a memory?

Once I did have a baby. A baby girl. Liz, I would have called her. Liz... like me, except I'm not really Liz, am I? I hadn't really known that until now- lodged, or trapped, in this bed-like tube with my head covered in probes by the alien. My... my story has yet to catch up to the present. My story...

Zaps of electricity force me back to the campsite with George only days ago...

Electricity...

Mom...

Grandpa...

Chad...

"Look George! Somebody was here before us."

"The guy you're looking for?"

"If we can just figure out which way he went."

"He had a campfire, but it was small; he didn't stick around long. It looks like he rushed off that way."

"How can you tell all of that?"

"He dropped some stuff over there."

"So, he got chased you think? Or was chasing?"

"Only one way to find out."

We followed the wrapper debris to footprints in the mud. George was busy tasting trees, for some beat-brain reason, so I snagged another apple and took off looking around. Weeks Cemetery was long ago the final resting place for many ancestors, but that place was no longer for people. There were few remains of headstones around, but rather the skeletal remains of something else covered most of the area. We stood before what looked like a shelled out main street that had been left to rot for hundreds of years; a city lost underwater only now to be rediscovered, the water drained but the damage maintained. The layout of the debris field was difficult to comprehend; it was huge, and old as the ground that had grown up around it. Trees grew through the gaps in the metal. My resolve was set, however, my confidence was low. Whatever it was, it was Chad's mystery; if I found him maybe I could get some answers, and stop worrying.

Inevitably, the trail ended. In a layout that reminisced a city block, the alien structures lined an open pathway. Several large building-sized frames clamored around, reaching towards open sky, scuttled husks of nothing any longer. Halfway up on the left side was a puddle of cackling water. It looked like the purest water ever, so clear you almost couldn't tell it was anything at all. Blue flames bubbled off the water's surface causing a frightening crackle as they slowly dissipated. From the puddle was a black char streak leading to a dog-sized char-chunk. We walked with utter trepidation. George looked at me and I nodded with pretend confidence. There was a lot of blood leading from the chunk into the distance. It was no dog.

Chad hacked off his right leg, mid-calf.

The blood led us right to the rest of

his corpse.

His face expired in pain. I could tell he had been crying, his eyes were bloodshot red and his cold cheeks still damp.

He died from the blood loss, I could tell it didn't take him long to bleed out.

Chad had stepped into the fire water, he hadn't seen it and stepped in deep, past his ankle. He decided to rend the flesh from his bone to escape the rising flames. He traveled at night it seemed. He knew the dangers. He was the one who told *me* about the floating, about the burning water, but only George had known about the bulgasari.

Ejected from the rooftop onto our pathway, the bulgasari looked wretched and even startled. George ran away. I wanted to run, but the monster caught my eyes in its gaze. It held an aggressively defensive posture, as if to ward us away. In the moment I was too scared to notice... but it acted like a mother protecting its children. Did those things have children?

It chased me into the hollow structures, fueled by an intense rage that

made lightening and smoke fume off her back
excessively. It crashed and careened through
strange metallic walls. The bulgasari's
movements were explosive, quick and short
leaps with crashing paws and jab-like
swipes.

She roared in an awful way, a way I
knew was desperation, but at the same time
reminded me of the moans and wails of all
the ones like Grandpa, dying together in the
most unnatural way.

George jumped from a cloud in the sky
firing several volleys from the torch as he
descended onto the bulgasari's back, then
stabbed her with a metallic shard the length
of his arm. The bulgasari didn't care much
when George stabbed it, in fact she seemed
to enjoy it at first, finally rising in a
violent twist and upwards thrust landing
George back on the ground. The torch slid
across the ground on impact and George shut
his eyes.

It loomed for several slow motion
moments as if to decide on how hurt it might
be. I noticed the torch nearby. The mother

of bulgasari stood stunned, but the lightening off its back burst with empowered force that channeled through the wreaked walls; the smoke made it seem like growing midnight. I grabbed the gun and shot the final bullet into its neck. The torch-light pellets burrowed their way through the carapace of the beast, dripping out of its under carriage in a slow race. It whimpered then collapsed, as everything else does when it dies. The metallic clank when the bullets dropped from holes in its belly onto the floor sounded like what I imagined when sunlight reflects off frozen water droplets long caught in the planet's orbit sounded like. There was a pleasant song-like quality to it, a tap-dance signifying the mother's death. I wondered if it haunted those hypothetical bulgasari pups left behind.

Crawled. Crawled. All alone he crawled, and crawled, and crawled, at least four devrons around the side of the bank. I selfishly wondered if Chad thought of me at all.

His last act, a scribbled note on blood
soaked paper and stolen ink:

This place fascinating
alien ship
It's technology.
We caused it, they came

𝔗𝔥𝔢 𝔏𝔞𝔰𝔱 𝔅𝔞𝔩𝔩𝔬𝔬𝔫

Chad died in agony during his efforts to uncover truth and history, to find answers to questions people long forgot to ask as humanity slipped backwards through melioration. As Liz decided to bury him I had to wrap up the remains and carry them over my shoulder until we found the spot where we dug the devron deep hole. We hung our heads and watched the sun-filled hole, leaves on the wind, orange and dry from weeping, no longer draped in emerald, discarded as the Torch was into the pit before we filled it in and covered it with a stone that bore no name.

When looked upon logically, one can

deduce that the nature of this world has been affected by the combination of alien influences and split atoms. A simple deduction, now, but why is this one location preserved? Are there other islands of preservation as well? My attempts to communicate this with Liz have failed. She's enamored by the apples, withdrawn into a mental cocoon.

Somewhere, over gradual time, we forgot the basis of our whole. *Anarchy loosed upon the world and everywhere the ceremony of innocence is drowned; the best lack conviction while the worst are full of passionate intensity,* was told to me in one of Sarawati's dreams by Michael Robartes. We seemed to stand on the shoulders of those who came before us, who stood on the shoulders and corpses of those before them. Are we humbled by any of it?

We found something special, though, something outside of what we thought possible. I'm not sure if Liz had figured it out yet, what Chad was looking for, but we'd found it.

The debris is from one of the three interstellar vehicles that landed on the Earth. The aliens had advanced far beyond humanity, yet were vulnerable; they failed to predict how mankind would cognate their arrival.

Liz was lost in mourning. We buried Chad's remains nearest where Liz thought her family's plot sat, that was the best we could do and I told her Chad would have liked it there.

After two days of silent camping at the grave, we went on to explore the area of the empty field beyond the grave. Liz was in a silent state of shock, blankly attempting to follow along as I careened forward. We went past the field, across a dingle, and into a thickly wooded area. Liz fell down a steep embankment and I followed her to find us on a shady path overgrown by trees; the sunlight that pierced the canopy was blemished green and gold.

An irrigation canal trickled across the path. It was perfectly straight, leading to an opening in the ground held open by mechanized debris. We walked and walked and walked into the black, I knew not why. Liz didn't say a word as she led us down the perfectly straight hall, she kept descending with no notion I was still there, and I stopped caring if we'd ever come back to reality. I could feel her pain and understood where her mind had gone; a circle of infinite quiets like when I carried pa.

Eventually I lost all feeling in my legs, but the path kept going as if we'd eventually reach the belly of the world, but I knew that wasn't possible so I wondered where it could possibly lead and if this is what we were supposed to be afraid of.

"You can hear it, can't you?" She muttered so softly I wasn't positive I'd imagined her in the first place. Our only source of light was a golden red mist of various densities throughout the air.

She wouldn't tell me what she heard, what was leading her, but after walking more k-devrons and still feeling as fresh as I did in the morning, we kept going. It didn't take long after that, we saw a light and reached a room.

"Ah, finally, you have arrived."

"Where are we?" Liz asked him with a calmness like I've never seen in her before, "What are you?" she spoke rhetorically as if to a child.

The room was larger than the whole of my childhood home. The curved walls formed a dome several sizes larger than the one dad and I saw distant weeks south of Boston[43] only this one was still intact and a mix of blue and white and green, with blinking purples and orange. The room appeared something like a workshop filled with broken devices both theirs and ours. The center of the room was filled with formed light images depicting the night sky. All the stars were crashing all over as I watched on with amazement.

"My name was ⚭⚭⚭⚭⚭, don't be scared Creatures," a holographic creature appeared in front of the stars and night, composed of

_____

43. The old capitol of the old world. Famous for its dome that depicted the night sky underneath and was used to observe the heavens as a symbol, a watchful eye of providence, that beamed like a lighthouse across the land.

114

the same wavelengths distinguished only by a
thick black outline uttered at us.

"What are you?"

"It helps, they dictate me Lois."

Lois seemed to toggle gloaming switches
and keys.

"How long have you been down here?"

"Two hundred years or more, can be what
I spent composing your species I at that
time, all. Don't expect to find a bit of
Sapient life."

I think it was a her, but like the
stars the luminescence flickered and had an
artificial air.

"You're not real, are you?"

Lois seemed irked by the term 'real'
and while it made no facial expression of
indication it did rapidly tap at buttons
with a sense of urgency.

"Holography is to separate the light
from the object can later write, and
construction technologies. It is used for
the transmission of three-dimensional images
as holograms. The hologram is an image, 3-
d."

A blue thick mist jet from the walls into our being, forced itself through our skin, forced us into a state similar to the time moments before falling asleep.

"Maybe there are moments, when possibility space of dream's humanity. Unfortunately, we have those dreams you short. You would have expected and our intention is to anxiety among people it had, people he reacts violently we are conversation expense? And anyway, it is our think following delays have shame."[44]

"I'm not sure I understand. George?" But I had not and could not say anything.

"Translation lexicon patching... voice protocol... adjusting... syntax errors... repairing. Your ancestors attacked us when we arrived."

"Had you not considered we would react

---

44 . Mastery over the human language took time to construct a practical vocal database: "Perhaps there was a time when humankind would dream of the possibilities of space. I'm sorry to say we've cut those dreams short... We didn't intend to frighten your people, we didn't expect your people to react so violently, self-sacrifice you call it? Either way, I am sorry that our coming has delayed humanity so much." After a few real-time exchanges I was able to fix the errors in my articulation.

in fear?" Liz was reforging her own mind.

"Your planet's transmissions were accidentally picked up by a probe network we sent into deep space. It was the first evidence of extraterrestrial sapient life. Deranged by this illumination we re-purposed several vessels and charted in your direction post haste. Our approach was not calculated; we expected you would be as impatient as we were to meet new life. The probability of alien life forms is high, that's true, but the vastness of the void made it seem like finding it would be dubious. The chemistry of life, that which makes fauna, are the most common elements in the universe. Life happens relatively quickly with the most abundant ingredients. But you were the first we had the chance to meet; the only species we knew where to find."

The alien went on and on. It spoke in a similar way as Saraswati in that it clearly had developed and accumulated knowledge over many years. We sat and listened to the words while deriving the shame and sorrow felt by

117

the creature. It- this digitized mind- had spent the last two centuries time trying to learn as much about humanity as possible.

"My solitary goal has been to preserve whatever I was able to of the human race. As I undertook this task I found that despite any success I might have, I would never be able to capture a significant picture of it all; the sheer diversity of culture and wonderful variations of on the dataset. I've done all I could. I've archived it all in the hope we can mend some of the damage. I've cloned several minds onto data storage here in the ship. One day others from my world will come and perhaps we can rebuild and forge ourselves a new future."

I told the mind about the apples and Saraswati. I asked if it knew about Iktomi, Dinesh, Yeomra, and if they were aliens, too. I needed to know if Lois had anything to do with that, how the apples made us smarter, how the trees could talk, and the bulgasari were eating all our past.

"That is unlikely."

"What is it then?"

"Allow me to take a scan. This machine will not hurt you, but will allow us to image your brain to better understand you. You both are the first live Refulgents I've met."

I climbed into a horizontal tube that softly ejected from the floor. It was so sleek, so beautiful, like an upright sarcophagi made of metal; like the barrel of a gun. The chamber was just larger than I with an inset the soma form of a human for me to rest in as the booth tilted prone. Even as I lay flat, through a small lunette peephole, I could watch the conversation between Liz and the alien computer.

"For over two hundred years of study and observation I have come to understand that the human lifetime has reduced to seventy approximate years provided healthy living."

"Your coming here did that?

"Our decent through your atmosphere triggered a response that we never expected-that you would be willing to incur self inflicted wounds to limit potential outcomes. But it wasn't just that. Something happened to us. It was a combination of weariness, deep space, and home sickness accumulated. Our stasis system's cascading errors built up that, while continually purged and reset, caused many of the population to go in and out of stasis many times more than was necessary. A systemic glitch caused variations of pressure and lower average perfusion of blood to the brain. Many of our leaders suffered transient ischemic attacks at first, coritcobasal degeneration and chronic ischemia developed commonly over the course of our journey."

"You've doomed us to a life only a quarter of what we deserve," Liz cried.

"Yes, and destroyed tens of million of my people. We came with great need for catharsis, dreams of ultimate possibility, to remedy a lingering toska. At least some of you have survived. Only six survived the crash on this ship and we built this representation of ⱯⱯꝊⱮꝊꞨ before they died. You can rebuild. There is hope."

"Chad's become nothing more than a memory."

"I'm still reconstructing human history from the sources I can access. When living, corporeal members of my species come they can aid in this endeavor and the reconstruction of all you've lost."

"You will never be able to understand our true loss, let alone give us back what we've lost."

The tube gave a low hum as it did the thing it was intended to do. I hoped that it would help us somehow. Through the glass I could see Liz, still weeping and engrossed in her memories, when suddenly thousands of images of people appeared before me, both of us and of them; I was no longer certain if time was real, or if those moments had lasted a second or a hundred years, whether there was a Liz or a Chad or a self and others. A thousand forms on the mirror surface, disappearing beneath each other and melting into each other, filled my view. They eventually vanished and I could see Lois smiled gently. I tried to properly fool

a smile back. Liz curved over on the floor
in a purely fetal position as another tube
rose up for her to enter. Uncontrollable
tears trickled down her childish face. She
was overwhelmed by the feelings of a great
love, a love forever lost. She curled
tightly into a ball, right down on the
ground, in front of the holographic alien
watching motionlessly, lifeless, whose
holographic smile reminded her of everything
that she had ever loved in her life, of
everything that had ever been of value.

Zero Again

All the Zeals are dead. First the Prime, then those who would try to be. Stasis failure caused hallucinations and aggression. Some of us survived the crash, initially, but we had yet to prepare for the atmosphere and available consumable materials. All the time getting here; all our hope and excitement. We should have done more, better. I fear all of us will die. I am in charge now and I've ordered all the power be reserved for the stasis. I will remain awake for as long as I can to ensure our survival and to collect data on-

and for-

Electroencephalography is a poor comparison for my imaging device. You know how well they could read and display the images of the mind, but in my time here, and with the weakness of the human brain, I've developed the ability to implant memories and information of my own.

The life on this refulgent blue orb, a

gem that seems valuable only because it is surrounded by filth in dead space, is all synthetic. Mere chemicals that react in simple and predictable manners have developed in cascading complexity to simulate consciousness. Their intellect, a biological and accidental mimic at low efficiency. Human beings are pretend; our way is everlasting. These human minds are like a defective, enfeebled pet, a dog barking at its bark. I've implanted within them knowledge of what we are.

This is the last transmission I will bother to send home. You will come here. Fail not as you've often done before. I'll soon be uploading the last of my mind into the ship's processors for you to find, as a beacon, with all the information I've been able to collect collated in the mean time.

When you come they will know our name and they will accept you from their knees.

— ÀꝊꝊꝊ

Acknowledgements

This novella would not exist if not for the hard work and support of Hollie DeFrancisco. I'd also like to thank Wells Fargo without whom the release would have come one year earlier. Finally, Dan, Mike, and Mike, D.J, and Terri – none of whom are reading this – all of whom I hope are writing still.

www.ingramcontent.com/pod-product-compliance
Lightning Source LLC
Chambersburg PA
CBHW021203130626
46554CB00005B/1965